Catty Corner

LANDS ON HER FEET

union
square
kids

NEW YORK

CHAPTER ONE

"**W**affles!" Catty Corner called as she tip-toed into the kitchen. "Where's my little mousy friend?"

Catty opened the refrigerator and looked inside. Waffles could be *anywhere*. "Yoo-hoo!" She peered into a bowl of cut-up watermelon. "Are you in here, Waffles?"

Waffles wasn't a *real* living, breathing mouse, but he was Catty's best friend. He was especially good at the hiding part of

1

hide-and-seek. Sometimes he hid in places where Catty wasn't allowed to go so she had to break the rule to find him, but it wasn't like that was her fault. (Her parents disagreed.)

She held her nose and popped her head in the trash can. "What about in here, Waffles? Come out, come out, wherever you are! Ewww! Is that last night's tuna salad?"

Catty looked around the kitchen until— "Aha!" she said as she noticed something pink hanging from the top of the refrigerator. It looked suspiciously like a tail.

Faster than you could say "nine lives," Catty leapt onto the counter and then on top of the refrigerator. Her fuzzy orange tail helped her balance like a secret agent ballerina.

Oh, it was dusty up here! Catty was sure Mom would want to know. Maybe that information would make it okay that Catty was definitely breaking a rule by being up here.

It was hard work being half-cat. Sure, regular cats lived the good life. They made up their own rules. But when you were half-cat, half-girl, grown-ups made rules you had to follow.

There were the big three that were especially important outside of the house:

- 🐾 No hissing.
- 🐾 No scratching.
- 🐾 No biting.

Then there were all the little ones that mattered at home:

- 🐾 No cat fights with Miss Taylor's grumpy old cat, Opie.

- 🐾 No midnight zoomies when Dad had work in the morning.
- 🐾 No jumping on top of refrigerators, counters, or lamps.
- 🐾 No knocking over shiny things, especially if it's just for fun.

The list was endless! And Waffles wasn't even up here. The pink tail she'd seen turned out to be a missing hair tie. Catty had broken a rule for no good reason. As she eyed the glittering crystal vase stored on top of the fridge, she knew she was in danger of breaking another.

It was as if Mom and Dad didn't even get that the best part of shiny things was knocking them over.

The sunlight from the kitchen window shined through the vase, creating a kaleidoscope of colors that Catty wished she could run right through.

Carefully, she crawled across the top of the fridge, closer to the vase. It was just so pretty!

"Catty! Corner! Get. Down. From. There. And don't you dare touch that vase!"

Uh-oh. Catty froze with one foot in midair. Mom was using *that* voice.

Catty's pointy ears folded down and her eyes went round as she tried her best to look innocent. "Moooom, I wasn't going to."

Then Catty gasped, suddenly remembering why she was up here in the first place. "I've got to find Waffles! We're playing hide-and-seek, and it's turned into a real game of cat-and-mouse, if you know what I mean."

Catty's mom's tail bristled like a bottle brush, which only meant one thing: She was paw-sitively *mad*.

"I love you..." Mom said, like it was a warning.

"I love you, too!" Catty sang as she wiggled her tail.

"But!"

"Uh-oh..."

"You and Waffles are driving me cattywampus!" Mom hissed.

Catty giggled, she couldn't help it. In her family, "cattywampus" meant losing all control, going totally wild, and tapping into your inner animal. Mom was mad, but she still sounded silly saying that word.

Just then, Catty's and Mom's ears twitched at the sound of keys jangling in the front door. Dad was home from work!

Catty's dad did not have pointy ears or a tail, but she and Mom loved him anyway. Even if his reflexes weren't that good. And his hearing wasn't as sharp. And he couldn't see that well at night and was always tripping over LEGO bricks. The chirping birds first thing in the morning didn't seem to bother him one bit. He slept right through.

Dad came into the kitchen carrying a big stack of pies from the Friends Hollow Pie Company, where he worked as a pastry chef and new recipe tester. "Hello! How are my favorite felines?"

Catty got a whiff of her favorite blueberry lemon pie and forgot about Waffles for just a second, until...

Catty spotted a streak of fur stuck to the top of Dad's knit cap. A little felt mouse.

"Waffles! There you are!" Catty said, and... pounced from her perch on the refrigerator.

"Catty! *No!*" said Mom with wide eyes.

"Catty—*wha?*" said Dad.

But Catty was already leaping through the air.

Catty landed on Dad, who went tumbling into Mom, spilling his pies and sending the three of them crashing to the floor in a big pile of arms, legs, and tails.

It was a cat-astrophe.

Above them, the vase wobbled. Catty couldn't look away. It tilted farther. It shimmered like a rainbow as it fell ... and ...

SMASH.

"Oops," said Catty. She licked a piece of blueberry lemon filling off her nose. "Mmm, tasty!"

"I thought so too," Dad said with a groan from underneath her.

Catty might have been half-cat, but that did not mean she always landed on her feet.

CHAPTER TWO

The next morning, Catty jumped out of one of her cat trees with a funny feeling racing up her tail. Catty's tail could warn her that something was happening—good or bad. It could be a dog around the corner or butterflies in the sky. Mom called it Tail Intuition.

Catty's ears perked up when she heard the kids across the street laughing.

She watched them from her window. They were playing with sidewalk chalk. It

12

looked like they were having fun drawing an alien spaceship full of dogs. That checked out. As far as Catty was concerned, dogs were from another planet.

The oldest boy, who had big front teeth and red hair, looked up and saw Catty staring. Catty recognized him. She'd seen him get on and off the school bus every day for the last few years. He pointed to her. All the other kids looked up with their jaws wide open. Some of them began to whisper.

Catty gasped and ducked down, embarrassed that she'd been caught spying.

This wasn't new. Catty didn't really know any other kids her age, but when she played outside or went for bike rides with Dad, kids in the neighborhood often whispered. Catty knew that being half-cat was more normal inside her house than it was outside it.

Catty sighed and got Waffles out of his little bed. She had made it for him using an empty sardine tin and socks that were too small for her. She got dressed, put Waffles in the front pocket of her overalls, and skipped downstairs for breakfast.

The Corner household was lined with bookshelves, plants, and prisms on the windows. There were cat trees and beds in every corner. For a half-girl, half-cat, it was basically a palace. Today the sun shined through the prisms, making colors dance on the floor. It was a perfectly good day to read a book and roll around in a patch of sunlight.

At the kitchen table, Mom and Dad looked unusually excited—like Christmas morning excited. Mom's tail whipped back and forth, and Dad hummed as he played a game on his phone. Catty's favorite breakfast sat steaming on her plate: a tuna omelet and a pile of cat-shaped pancakes. Catty's nose twitched with suspicion. Something was up. She'd felt it in her tail earlier, and now this.

"What's going on?" Catty demanded. "Wait a second. Is it my birthday? Did I forget?"

"No birthdays today, but we've got some *big* news, Catty," said Dad. "Your mom got her dream job at the fish cannery!"

Catty's ears shot straight up and her eyes bugged out. "Wait. Does that mean unlimited tuna?"

Mom's smile was a bit tight, and her ear twitched. "Yes, but . . ."

Catty's tail puffed out. Oh no. Not another *but.* "But *what?*"

Mom held Catty's hand. "That means I won't be home during the day anymore."

Well, that didn't sound like exciting news, after all. "So that means I'll be home all alone. . . . What if the doorbell rings and I hide under the couch? Or Mr. Allister's dog digs under the fence again and chases me up a tree? What if Opie the cat tries to kidnap Waffles?" The thought made her want to hiss!

"Catty, we're not leaving you home alone all day. We would never do that," said Dad. "You'll be starting third grade! In a real school. With other kids!"

Other kids? Like the kids across the street? Catty sank down in her chair, her tail swishing anxiously. Suddenly breakfast didn't look so yummy anymore. She probably should have just stayed in her cat tree.

Mom had always been Catty's teacher. Together, they learned all of Catty's favorite subjects, like reading, history, and string-chasing. Catty had only seen real school on TV and in movies. One time she'd volunteered with her parents at a canned food drive at Friends Hollow Elementary. She had been amazed by the ultra-big ropes course in the gym and all the fancy water fountains she dreamed of pawing at.

But the idea of all those human kids made her nervous, especially when she remembered the boy across the street pointing at her. "I don't know, Mom. What if I just stayed home? I won't answer the door

for strangers, and if Mr. Allister's dog gets out, I can call him and—"

Dad laughed. "Oh, I don't think—"

"Cats, even half-cats, can be *very* independent," Catty said. She could convince her parents. She'd never lost an argument with Waffles. "Leave some snacks out and—"

"You know we can't do that, sweetie," Mom said in a no-nonsense voice.

Catty's mind raced like it was chasing a laser pointer. What would the kids at school be like? Would they like playing games, like throwing felt mice up in the air with their feet? What kind of naps did they take (short? long? belly-up? belly-down?)? Catty had three friends already: Mom, Dad, and Waffles. She didn't think she needed any more.

Still, she'd always suspected she was missing out on things like field trips and birthday parties and recess.

"What do you think, Kitty-Cat?" Dad asked. "Are you ready to start school on Monday morning?"

Catty sighed so hard, some of her hair blew up in the air. "Do I have a choice?"

Mom and Dad shook their heads no.

Catty looked down at Waffles in her pocket, wishing for once that there was something he could say to make her feel better.

CHAPTER THREE

It was the night before her first day of school, and Catty could not sleep.

For the last few years, Catty had watched the school bus drive up and down her street every morning and every afternoon. It was bright yellow, like a big goldfish, and was always full of kids laughing and shouting. Would the noise hurt Catty's super-sensitive cat ears? Would her new teacher do all the funny voices in her favorite stories, like

Mom did? What if her rainbow ball of yarn rolled under the bookshelf and her teacher couldn't reach it?

Most of all, Catty worried about being different. In all the books she'd read about school, there were never *any* half-cat girls. Not a single one! What if the other kids thought she was weird? What if they made fun of her ears and yanked on her tail? What if she made no friends at all, like Miss Taylor's cat, Opie, who spent all day sleeping on the porch and hissing at everything and everyone? No one wanted to be friends with a hissy kitty!

Waffles was tucked into his sardine tin bed on Catty's nightstand. She turned on her side to face him. "Hey, buddy, what if ... what if no one at school knew I was half-cat? What if I could hide my tail and ears? Wouldn't that make things easier?"

Waffles was very still and looked like he was thinking very hard.

Catty nodded. "You're right. It's not an easy decision."

Behind Waffles's bed was a cleaned-out tuna can full of doll clothes Catty had saved for him. Scarves, hats, jackets . . .

"A hat *would* hide my ears," Catty said. "And I bet I could tuck my tail into my shirt. Hmm . . ." She flopped over onto her back. Tomorrow felt like a big surprise, and cats *hated* surprises. (Well, unless they were happy surprises like going to get snow cones, or a trip to the bookstore.)

When she couldn't stop worrying, Catty decided to dash up and down the stairs for some midnight zoomies, which always made her feel better. (Doing zoomies at midnight was technically against the rules, but Catty was sure that Mom and Dad would understand this one time. This was a zoomies emergency!)

Catty dragged her nails down the back of the sofa. Ahhhh, that felt nice.

All the furniture at Catty's house had her claw marks on it, so Mom didn't mind her tearing around. Catty wasn't allowed to scratch other people or their things, but the furniture at home was already full of claw marks from her and Mom, and Catty liked it that way. It reminded Catty that this was her home, where everything was safe. Even sharp claws.

As she slid down the banister one last time, Catty's nerves finally settled. Tomorrow was the big day and she would need a full night's sleep to put her best paw forward.

With a big yawn, Catty made herself cozy on a fresh pile of warm towels in the laundry room. She really could sleep anywhere. That was one thing she and Dad did have in common.

The next morning, Catty's mother helped her put on her jacket.

"Do you remember the big three rules?" Mom asked.

Catty nodded seriously. "No hissing, no scratching, no biting."

"Good kitty," said Mom. "Okay, let's go! It's a big day for *both* of us!"

Catty pulled on the knit hat she'd decided to wear and tucked her tail under the
back of her sweater.

"Catty, why are you hiding your ears
and tail?" Mom asked.

Catty bit her lip. "I thought, well, maybe for the first day, I wouldn't share my catty side," she said. She wasn't ashamed of her cattiness. Mom and Dad had raised her to be proud of it.

And Catty was proud to be half-cat. Well, not *technically* half. Mom was part-cat, and then so was her mom, and then her mom before her. Catty hadn't done the family cat tree math, but Mom's side of the family was full of fuzzy ears and swishy tails, so that was what mattered. But when it came to school, Catty just wanted to fit in. At least, at first.

Mom's face scrunched in a way that told Catty she had a lot of opinions even if she wasn't saying them out loud. "Well, if you're not comfortable showing your cat side just yet, that's okay. You decide what parts of yourself you share. But, Catty," Mom said, "hats aren't allowed in classrooms."

"They're not?"

This was not a happy surprise.

"No," Mom said gently. "You'll have to take your hat off once you get to school."

Catty's tail drooped.

Mom frowned. "Do you want me to call the principal?"

"I don't want to make it a big deal—"

"Catty," Mom said, looking at her with sparkling green eyes, "it's never a bad thing to ask for what you need. Okay?"

Mom always knew the right thing to say. "Okay, Mom!"

Catty waved goodbye to Waffles. He was sitting in the windowsill so he could see the bus, too. *Now* Catty was ready for her first day of school.

CHAPTER FOUR

At the bus stop, it was so windy that everyone had to hold on to their hats and coats. Catty's beanie itched on her ears, which were plastered to the sides of her head. She hated when anything touched her ears. Maybe the hat wasn't such a good idea. Too late now.

"No hissing, no scratching, no biting," Catty muttered to herself. "No hissing, no scratching, no biting."

A girl with a huge purple backpack and big floppy curls in pigtails spotted Catty. "Oh! Are you new? You look familiar. Did you just move here? Have you been to our school's library yet? Did you know you can check out books *and* craft supplies?"

Whoa! Talk about information overload. "Yeah, I'm new," Catty said, feeling her tail twitch beneath her clothes. "I'm starting today."

"I'm Jo! My mom bought me Band-Aids that look like bacon. Look!" Jo rolled up her sleeve and showed off a printed bandage that looked like a slab of bacon wrapped around her elbow.

Catty recoiled. She preferred tuna. But Jo didn't seem to notice.

"I was the new girl once. Is that beanie one hundred percent wool? Because it'll shrink if you put it in the dryer, you know. One time, I threw my brother's dinosaur sweater in the dryer and now it fits my dolls. He was so mad but he always said that sweater was itchy and . . ."

Catty had never met anyone who talked so much or so fast. Jo was as bouncy as a rabbit! She reminded Catty of her favorite crinkly tinsel ball, the one that sparkled and never bounced in the direction you expected it to.

Catty wanted so badly to swat at one of Jo's springy pigtails, but she curled her hands into fists and stopped herself. It may not have been one of Mom's rules, but Catty was pretty sure that swatting at Jo wouldn't make a good first impression.

When Jo paused for a moment to take a breath, Catty said, "I'm Catty, by the way."

Right then, a huge gust of wind caught everyone by surprise. It yowled down the street and blew Catty's hat clean off.

"Nooooo!" Catty cried as she chased after her hat and just barely caught it. She tried to cover her ears, but it was too late. Unleashed, they sprang straight up. *Boing!*

"No *way,*" said Jo, her mouth a perfectly round O. "Are those *cat* ears? Are they real?"

"Y-yes?" said Catty. "I mean, yes! They're my real ears. You could say they're . . . *fur* real." Catty snorted at her own joke.

"That's . . . so . . ."

Catty cringed. She wished she could unsay her corny joke.

"*Cool!*" said Jo. "Oh my goodness, I love cats. I wish *I* had cat ears. My ears are so boring. One day I want to get them pierced, like my sister. She's six feet tall! But before you ask, she hates basketball. One time on a family camping trip . . ."

Catty put her hat in her backpack and wiggled her ears. That was unexpected. Maybe there was nothing to worry about after all. Maybe Jo could be Catty's first fully human real-life friend. (No offense, Waffles!)

Just then, the school bus pulled up to the curb. *No hissing, no scratching, no biting. No hissing, no scratching, no biting.*

"Have a wonderful day, Catty!" Mom called from the porch in her brand-new cannery uniform.

For a moment, Catty wanted to run back to her and go home. But she knew she had to be brave. It was meow or never. She winked at Waffles, who watched from the window. Good or bad, she'd have plenty to tell him later today!

Catty fell in line behind Jo, and every-one climbed aboard.

Whoa! The bus was chaos, with too much to see, hear, and smell. The engine juddered and kids laughed and talked... and definitely not with their inside voices. Paper airplanes zoomed, and someone was waving a ribbon like a flag. Catty smelled gasoline and rubber erasers and a girl eating a donut in the back row. Catty's ears went flat, and she wished more than ever that she could run back home to Waffles.

This was much too much!

She scrambled down the aisle, worried she might go cattywampus.

All of a sudden, everything went quiet. *Whew!*

Then Catty realized why. Everyone was looking at *her*. They'd obviously never seen a girl with cat ears before. And they hadn't even seen her tail yet.

The bus doors sealed shut with a menacing *hissssss*.

Before Catty and Jo had even sat down, the giant goldfish began to chug down the road. Now Catty had another problem.

Not only did the bus look like a goldfish, but suddenly Catty felt like she was under water too. She could barely walk straight, and all the movement made her tummy feel funny.

"Whoa!" Jo said, giggling as she tried to keep her balance.

Balance was Catty's specialty, but even she got rattled when she was bouncing all over the place.

Jo finally noticed. "What's wrong, Catty? Your ears are all flat."

"I hate riding in cars," Catty said. "Turns out, buses are even worse!"

"Is that a cat thing?" Jo asked. "Well, my grandma's cat, Muffy, hates riding to the vet. Every time she gets in the car she'll yowl and yowl and yowl—" Jo stopped as Catty swayed. "Sorry, I'm not helping."

"What does your grandma do for Muffy?"

"She usually puts her in a crate."

Catty's stomach lurched. She definitely didn't want to ride to school in a crate. "I think I'll try sitting."

"My little brother gets carsick, and he says sitting over the wheel is too bumpy, so let's go over here."

Once she and Jo found a seat near the middle, Catty felt much better.

A boy with large teeth and red hair spun around in the seat in front of them. It was the boy from across the street!

"Hey!" he said. "I see you from across the street sometimes. Are you really some kind of cat?"

"Um . . ." Here went nothing. "Technically I'm half-cat."

The boy wasn't happy with that answer. "So are you an animal or a person?"

"She doesn't have to answer you if she doesn't want to, Milo," Jo said. Jo could do an excellent sassy mouth pucker.

"Or is that a costume?" Milo popped up in his seat. "It's not even Halloween yet."

Before Catty could stop him, he reached for her ears with a grubby hand. "Are those real?"

Catty didn't like her ears touched unless she felt very comfortable. And right now, Catty was *not* comfortable.

It all happened so fast. She let out a loud *hisss* and swatted at Milo's hand.

"Ow! What'd you do that for?" Milo pulled back his hand.

"I'm sorry!" said Catty. She hadn't meant to hurt him. She hadn't even touched him, not really.

"Heeeeelp!" Milo screeched, melting back into the seat.

"You started it, Milo! *Never* touch anyone without permission, especially not their hair. Or their ears!" Jo snapped. "It's called body boundaries! Look it up!"

"You all knock it off back there!" the bus driver shouted.

Catty covered her eyes with her hands. This was not good. *No hissing, no scratching, no biting.* Only five minutes into her new life and she'd already broken one of Mom's rules and come much too close to breaking a second.

The bus grew louder and louder as Catty quietly reached into her backpack for her hat. Maybe today would be easier if she could blend in, no matter what Jo said.

CHAPTER FIVE

Catty's teacher, Mr. Grole, had shaggy brown hair and a thick beard, and he kept patting his stomach. He looked more like a bear than a third-grade teacher.

Catty wasn't sure what to think of him, but her tail tensed every time he walked by.

"Catty Corner," Mr. Grole called, his voice deep. "Could you please come to my desk?"

"If I have to," she mumbled. Catty's tail threatened to puff out of her sweater as she walked to the front of the room. *No hissing, no scratching, no biting.*

There was a super-cute goldfish with a black spot shaped like a heart in a big glass bowl on Mr. Grole's desk. Catty had always wanted a pet fish, but Mom didn't think it was a good idea. Catty wondered what its name was. But Mr. Grole was staring at her as he scratched behind his ear, so Catty decided to ask later.

"Am I in trouble?" she whispered. "Was it because of what happened with Milo—"

Suddenly Mr. Grole smiled. It was a nice smile, even if he did have surprisingly large canines. "Catty! Of course not. I just wanted to introduce you to the class. I know it's not easy to join a class after the school year has already started, but a warm welcome is a Friends Hollow Elementary tradition!"

Catty's tail relaxed, and so did her ears under her hat. "Oh! That's okay with me then." She was nervous about standing up in front of everyone, but at least she wasn't in trouble. Yet.

"Also, Catty," Mr. Grole said, "your mother shared with me that you're half-cat." Catty appreciated that he spoke quietly. "That's wonderful. I know you may not see many other kids with cat ears and tails around here, but everyone is different and everyone is welcome. It's completely up to you whether or not you want to share your feline half with the class today. Though you should know that the school mascot is the bobcat, so you might be pretty popular around here." He made a paw with his hand.

She smiled. Maybe Mr. Grole was a cat person!

Before Catty could decide what she wanted to share with the class, a sound—like a fire alarm combined with Mom's egg timer—clattered and clanged through the room. Catty was so surprised, she almost jumped up onto the ceiling tiles and held on for nine lives.

"It's okay, Catty," Mr. Grole said. "That's the bell announcing the start of the school day. There will be another one at lunch, and again when it's time to go home."

Catty wasn't sure she liked the sound of that, but none of the other kids seemed bothered by the bell.

"Okay, okay, settle down, everyone," Mr. Grole called out. "One, two, three, eyes on me! You may have noticed that we have a new student with us today. Please welcome Catty Corner to our third-grade class."

Catty waved. She hoped everyone would like her, like Jo did, or at least give her a chance. Then she saw Milo in the back row, wearing a big pouty frown and cradling his hand like he was actually hurt. She tried smiling at him, but it felt too much like when Opie bared his teeth, and totally uncool.

"Why does *she* get to wear a hat and no one else can?" asked a boy in the front row, who had short blond hair and *no* cat ears.

"Yeah!" said the girl who sat behind Catty. "I wasn't allowed to wear my sun hat last year."

"It's not fair," another said.

"I have to brush my hair *every* day," one student moaned. "Can I start wearing a hat too?"

Mr. Grole stood and crossed his arms. "Settle down, everyone. Catty has special permission to wear her hat."

"But why?" the first boy moaned.

Catty knew that Mr. Grole couldn't answer his question without giving her away.

Milo smirked at the back of the room. "Yeah, why doesn't Catty tell us why she gets special treatment?"

From the front row, Jo gave Catty a smile so big that it made her whole face scrunch up. What if everyone was as cool with half-cats as Jo was?

Suddenly, Catty knew what she should do, and it didn't even take Tail Intuition to figure it out. Hiding felt comfortable—cats *loved* hiding. But people would find out sooner or later anyway. If she wanted to get to know her classmates, she had to give them a chance to get to know her.

Catty yanked off her hat and let her tail curl out from underneath her sweater. Woo! That felt good. "Meow," she said with a nervous giggle.

The whole class was so quiet, Catty could hear a dog barking six blocks over. Could someone just say something? Anything? Any minute now would be good!

She waited for everyone to freak out or be rude, but instead most of Catty's classmates looked more . . . curious.

"Can you hear really well?" asked a girl with her hair slicked back into a bun with pink feathers sticking out. Her pencil case read *Bebe*.

"I can actually hear a dog barking right now a few blocks away," Catty said. "Sounds like he's ready to go back inside!"

"Can you make your tail move?" the boy next to Jo asked.

Catty nodded and let her tail curl around her legs for her classmates to see.

"Can you climb walls?" another girl asked. "My cat totally climbs walls."

Catty laughed. "If they're soft!"

"If I'm allergic to cats, will I be allergic to you?" said a sniffly girl next to Jo. "I'm allergic to everything from nuts to grass."

"My dad's allergic to cats," Catty said, "and he's just fine with me and my mom."

"Your mom is half-cat too?" a girl with a giant orange bow on her head asked.

Catty shrugged. "I guess you could say it runs in the family."

"Can you see ghosts?" another boy asked. "My grandma says her cat Benjamin sees ghosts."

"Oh no," Catty said. "I hope I never do! Unless they're friendly."

A few kids laughed at her joke, and Catty had to admit that felt pretty cool.

"Okay, class, let's not put Catty on the spot too much," Mr. Grole said. "There will be plenty of time to get to know our new classmate."

Catty walked back to her desk like the classroom was her own personal catwalk. Her tail proudly swished from side to side. All the friendly faces and nice questions made it easy to ignore the couple of kids who gave her ugly looks, including Milo, who seemed just about ready to growl.

No hissing, no scratching, no biting, Catty reminded herself as she passed his desk.

"Okay class," Mr. Grole said, "yesterday we were talking about our local environment." He pulled a big map of the town of Friends Hollow over the chalkboard. And then . . . *Oh no.*

Catty sat up straight in her chair, her ears at attention.

Mr. Grole had a laser pointer. At home, Catty *loved* laser pointers. They made her go absolutely cattywampus. Totally feral! But this was not exactly the best time for laser chasing. *Breathe, Catty. It's just a bright little red light that zooms all over, begging to be caught. It's no big deal. It's no—*

He turned it on. The little red dot shined right on Otter Cove.

Catty's eyes zoomed across the map, following the glowing dot. *Pssst, pssst, pssst, try and catch me*, said the little dot.

"Who can tell me what I'm pointing to?" Mr. Grole asked.

Catty felt jumpy and anxious, and it wasn't because she knew the answer. A little voice in her brain said that if she was just fast enough, she might just catch the laser and then—

Mr. Grole moved the pointer all around in speedy circles. "Anyone? Come on, guys!"

Stay cool, Catty. Stay cool! She started to sweat as her eyes bounced up and down like a gymnast, following the laser. Catty's head snapped back and forth as she gripped her desk, trying to keep it together.

"What about over here?" Mr. Grole quickly zigzagged the laser to the Friends Hollow Dog Park.

That was too much. The dog park! She hissed (again!) and leapt to her feet. Catty was off like a slingshot, chasing after the laser. She zoomed across the classroom and scrambled after the little red dot, right to the top of Mr. Grole's map.

She almost had it!

Why was that dot always so fast? Time to go into cattywampus turbo mode!

Catty tore through the paper with a very satisfying *rip* and a big *slash*. What a great noise. It was total catnip to her brain! *Rip, rip, riiiiiiiiiiiiip. Shred, shred, shred!* And once she started, she simply couldn't stop until the entire thing was in tattered pieces.

Catty stood in the middle of a pile of Friends Hollow. The piece with City Hall on it fluttered down from the ceiling and brushed her nose, making it twitch.

"Oops," said Catty as she twisted her hands together.

Now that Catty could think clearly, she realized the entire class was laughing. Her spirits began to sink. Almost everyone had

been so nice, but look at what she'd done!
There was no way she could fit in now. Even
Jo looked confused.

"My map!" Mr. Grole said. Her teacher
didn't look so friendly anymore. Instead, he
was very, very disappointed.

Catty picked a chunk of Polk Avenue out
of her hair. She should have never come to
school. She'd already hissed *and* scratched.

And the school day wasn't over yet!

CHAPTER SIX

If anything could turn around Catty's bad day, it was lunch. She missed Mom, Dad, and Waffles so much. Hopefully Mom's homemade food would cheer her up. Catty's stomach growled, but at least it didn't hiss.

Inside Catty's lunch box was a note:

Dear Catty,
I know today will be filled with lots of new experiences, but I hope this lunch makes you feel right at home.
Love,
Mom ⩾♡⩽

Mom always knew just what to say—and pack.

Inside each compartment of Catty's colorful bento lunch box were Catty's absolute must-haves, including a mini milk carton and her very favorite food: anchovies.

She opened the tin can and closed her eyes as she took a big fishy whiff. YUM!

"Ewwww!" said a girl on the other side of the table as she held her nose.

Dad called anchovies "an acquired taste," but that didn't make any sense to Catty. She could eat anchovies like they were potato chips. Oh! Anchovy-flavored potato chips! Now, that was an a-meow-zing idea.

Beside her, Jo smiled encouragingly, even though she didn't look as sure about Catty's lunch as she had about her ears. Inside Jo's lunch box were five baby carrots, a heart-shaped peanut butter sandwich, and a chocolate pudding cup decked out with rainbow sprinkles. It looked good, but was definitely missing something fishy.

"That's so yuck," Milo said to Catty.

Catty's ears flattened. *No hissing, no scratching, no biting.* She didn't belong here, just like her anchovies. To distract herself from the way Milo made her feel, she kneaded her fingers on her legs under the table where nobody could see.

"Actually," said the girl from class with her hair in a bun with pink feathers, "that looks quite appetizing." She looked at Catty over her red glittery glasses. With her long arms and legs, she almost reminded Catty of a flamingo. "We eat with the eyes first, you know."

"We do?" said Catty. "I just use my mouth."

"Then we eat with our noses," the girl continued. "Smell is a big part of taste."

"That makes...sense." Catty gave an exaggerated wink. "Get it?"

But the girl was already laughing. She angled her own bento lunch box toward

Catty. "Mother always packs me sushi with soy sauce. I'm Bebe, by the way. Would you like to trade a bit?"

Catty had never tried soy sauce, but, like Mom said, this was a day for new experiences. And this new experience smelled pretty yummy. "Thanks. I'm Catty."

"I know," Bebe said, like she was the kind of person who knew a little bit of something about everything. "I think your hat is *très chic*. Your ears, too."

"Really?" Catty wasn't sure what Bebe meant by that, but the way she said it, it seemed like a compliment. And she really seemed to enjoy Catty's anchovies.

Catty looked over at Milo and whispered, "Take that!"

Feeling a little bit better about her lunch, Catty put her anchovies in her bowl and added a little soy sauce, too. The combination was delicious! Like fireworks for the taste buds!

"I can't wait for the book fair tomorrow," Jo said. "I'm going to buy *all* the journals. Give them to me. All of them! I need journals like zombies need brains!"

"A book fair?" Catty's tail whipped around with excitement. She didn't bother to hide it this time.

Jo nodded. "They set it up in the library and there are tables full of books to buy. Like I said, there's journals."

"And stickers, too," Bebe chimed in as she expertly balanced her chopsticks between her fingers. "But I have what I call sticker anxiety. What if I stick it on something that's suddenly gone out of style? There's no re-sticking a sticker."

Jo shrugged. "I've never met a sticker I couldn't stick."

Dad took Catty to the public library twice a month, and the whole family loved going to the bookstore, too, though it was a long car ride away from home. But a book fair right down the hallway? With books, journals, and stickers? This was too good to be true! Waffles would be so jealous.

"I have leftover birthday money that is begging to be spent," Catty said. "Do you like to read?"

"Um, more than a bird likes to chirp!" Jo laughed. "I write, too, if you didn't pick up on that. Which is why I collect journals. In this one story I'm working on . . ."

Catty's tail swept across the floor as she listened to Jo and imagined how many books she could get her paws on at the book fair. Then—"*MeOOOWWWWWWWWW!*" Catty screeched.

Someone had stepped on her tail!

Without thinking, Catty let out a loud *hiss* and bit down on the closest thing to her mouth. All she wanted was to make the pain go away. *Ouch, ouch, ouch, ouch, ouch!*

Except the thing in her mouth just so happened to be Bebe's hand.

"*Youch!*" Bebe screeched, and lunged back like she was scared of Catty. Her eyes were confused and full of hurt.

Catty gasped and pulled her tail into her lap. "I'm so, so sorry!"

Bebe held her hand. She blinked quickly, but that didn't stop the tears from falling down her cheeks.

Catty shrank down in her seat, trying to make herself as small as she could. She didn't mean to react like that. Surely whoever stepped on her tail did it by accident. Catty couldn't help her instincts. Sometimes they were great, like Tail Intuition. Other times? Not so much.

Then she noticed the uncomfortable silence. Catty looked around to all the surprised faces at the lunch table, except for Milo. His lips curled into a smug smile, like every bad thing he thought about Catty

had turned out to be true. And maybe he was right.

Mr. Grole, who was working lunch duty, walked over and shook his shaggy head. "Catty," he said, arms crossed, "come with me to the principal's office."

The principal's office? On her first day? *You've got to be kitten me!*

The rules had gone straight out the window. She'd broken the big three. *No hissing, no scratching, no biting.*

Now Catty was in serious trouble.

CHAPTER SEVEN

With her head hung low and her ears drooping down, Catty sat in the principal's office, wedged between Mom and Mr. Grole.

Mom had been called to the school. Even though Catty had missed her, this was a terrible reunion. It was Mom's first day too, and Catty had ruined it for both of them. By the sound of her disappointed huffs, Mom agreed.

Principal Pluck had a long nose, like a pelican, and her glasses perched at the very tip. "I think we can all agree this was a big misunderstanding," she said.

"Is Bebe okay?" Catty asked. Surely Bebe had to know it was an accident, right?

"She visited the nurse and is feeling just fine," Mr. Grole said. He didn't seem mad anymore. In fact, he looked a little worried . . . which was worse. Catty didn't like it when grown-ups looked worried. That meant the problem was so big that not even they knew how to fix it.

Mom looked at Catty with narrowed eyes. "I think it's important that Catty apologizes to Bebe when she has the chance to."

Catty nodded. She should have said sorry about a million more times. She felt so, so bad and wished she could make it all better *right now.*

"We agree," said Principal Pluck, "but it's already been a long day. Maybe Catty should go home for now and come back tomorrow? Take a pause and let everyone calm down. Tomorrow will be a fresh start."

"I guess I'll have to take the rest of the day off," Mom said with a frown, "but I think Principal Pluck is right."

Catty hated to leave early. She wanted to make it work, check on Bebe, and prove she had what it took to go to school. If she left now, that meant meanies like Milo were right: She was just a hissy kitty with no business going to school.

"What do you think about that, Catty?" Mom asked.

Catty slouched in her seat with a pout. At least if she went home, that meant she could catch Waffles up on all the drama, and oh, did Waffles *love* drama.

"We knew group school would be a big change, and change can take time. Let's start fresh in the morning. Okay, Catty?" Principal Pluck prompted.

Even though Catty didn't think she could show her face tomorrow morning after leaving like this, she nodded in agreement. It would take some work to claw her way back. She didn't know if she could do it. But maybe it would be worth it. At the very least, she needed to explain herself to Bebe, even if she never showed her face again at school.

"That's the spirit, Catty!" Mr. Grole said. He looked like he was about to pat her on the shoulder, but he changed his mind, like someone who is going to rub a cat's belly but then realizes what a bad idea that is.

"Hey, Mr. Grole?" Catty asked.

"Yes, Catty?"

"What's your fish's name?"

"Why? Are you looking for a snack?" he asked with a wink.

Catty blushed. "No, not like that. He's just cute is all."

"His name is Douglas Snickerdoodle."

Catty smiled. Thinking about their class pet almost made her want to go back to Mr. Grole's classroom. *Almost.* But the feeling didn't last.

CHAPTER EIGHT

When Catty got home, Opie was sleeping on their porch. As Catty stepped over him, he reached up and clawed at her tail.

He messed with the wrong kitty today! Catty hissed at the chubby gray cat and darted inside before he could hiss back.

"Catty!" her mom called after her, and then turned to Opie. "Time to go home, mister."

"I want to be alone," Catty shouted as she took Waffles off the windowsill and then slammed her bedroom door.

Catty plopped down in her fluffiest cat bed with her belly up. She and Waffles watched the puffy white clouds float across the clear afternoon sky outside the window. Normally, she loved being quiet and letting her imagination turn the clouds into shapes like strawberries or goblins. But she had to admit: Today it felt lonely.

After a while, Mom came to Catty's door with catnip shortbread cookies. Just one whiff made Catty's tail curl. She reached for the plate.

"Are you ready to talk now?" Mom asked.

"I admit defeat," Catty declared with her mouth full of shortbread. "Half-felines and school go together like cats and dogs. It's impossible."

Catty knew she had to do *something* with her days. Mom had her job. Maybe Catty could work at the cannery too. Or go to the bakery with dad. She was excellent at kneading dough.

Mom sat down beside her. Her tail was fluffier and a little lighter than Catty's. It wrapped around Catty tightly, even more comforting than a hug. "Catty, I know today was a doozy."

"A doozy?" Catty asked. "It was a *disaster*. Today will go down in *hissssstory* as the worst first day of school ever."

Mom laughed a little. She didn't seem as disappointed as she had been in Principal Pluck's office. "I have something very special to give you that I think might help."

"More than the catnip cookies?"

"Yes, the cookies were just a bonus." Mom smiled. "It's something I've been saving for you, and I hope it will make your second day at school a little easier."

"My *second* day?" Catty said. "Mooooooom. I can't go back there!"

"Oh yes you can, and you will," Mom said. "I really think this might help you feel differently."

Before Catty could protest again, Mom handed Catty a fuzzy pale lavender ... book? Catty immediately thought of Jo, and how excited she seemed about her journals.

This one said SCRATCH PAD across the front in hand-stitched letters.

"What is it?" Catty asked.

"This is my old diary from when I first started going to school. Before that, it was Granny Tabby's."

Just thinking about Granny Tabby made Catty's tail puff. Granny owned a yarn store a few towns over called Nine Lives Knitting Supplies. Despite being the oldest person Catty had ever met, Granny Tabby was always smiling and had the best style. She wore bright knitted scarves and matching leg warmers. She always scooped Catty right off the ground whenever she visited.

"All the stories from your granny's school days really helped me get through my own tough days." Mom laughed. "And you think you had a bad first day . . . just wait until you read some of my stories. There's some real cringeworthy stuff in there, kiddo. Maybe you could even add some diary entries of your own."

"You're letting me read *your* diary? Isn't that kind of personal?" Catty couldn't hide the excitement in her voice. Her mom's diary? Talk about a juicy read!

"There's not much I wouldn't share with you. Even the last slice of my favorite sardine pizza."

Catty liked the feel of the warm, fuzzy journal resting in her lap. And "Scratch Pad"? She liked the sound of that, too. It made her feel like she could pick up a pen and really let loose on the pages inside.

Without waiting a second longer, she opened the book and began to read.

Dear Diary,

Today was my first day of school. I liked the tuna sandwich in the cafeteria, but it wasn't as good as Mama's. Everything was going just dandy until I got sleepy after lunch.  The sun hit my desk just right, and I couldn't help but use my tail as a pillow and take a little catnap. Miss Crouch was NOT pleased. Then a bird teased me at the window and I wanted to go out and play with it so badly. I pawed at the glass and everyone got distracted.

Mama said I should write down my feelings when I get overwhelmed, and she even sewed fabric around this notebook so when I'm feeling extra frisky, I can let my claws out.

She says it's okay if I jump, or do something I'm not supposed to . . . No one's perfect. I just have to land on my feet.

Writing this down did make me feel better. And maybe tomorrow will be okay! I've got my tail crossed!

> Hugs and Meows,
> Tabby

"There are lots more entries just like that in there," Mom said. "Why don't you read for a little bit? I'll call you when dinner is ready."

Nobody had to tell Catty to read twice. Finally, something she was good at! She climbed to the very top of her favorite cat tower and settled in. Being so high up in the air felt safe. She liked the feeling of looking down on her room, like everything down there was suddenly small, including her problems.

Catty curled up with the journal and began to read.

Holy fishsticks! She couldn't even believe all the stories in this journal. One time, Mom got hairballs during a class birthday party and coughed one up right on the cake. Another time, Granny Tabby got chased by a dog across the playground and had to hide up in a tree and missed a pop quiz. The fire department had to come and rescue her!

Okay, maybe Catty's day hadn't been a *total* disaster in comparison.

If Mom and Granny Tabby had gone through the same kind of impawssible stuff when they were growing up, maybe Catty could try just *one* more day at school. She glanced across the room at the jar where she kept all her loose change and birthday money. At the very least, checking out the book fair would be worth it.

CHAPTER NINE

The next morning, Catty waited at the bus stop with her ears proudly out, her Scratch Pad safe in her backpack, and her tail swishing with excitement. She even wore a T-shirt that said *Cat Hair, Don't Care.*

"You want me to wait with you, Kitty-Cat?" Mom asked before they said goodbye.

Catty shook her head. "I think I've got it under control!"

Mom smiled. "Remember. No hissing, no scratching—"

"No biting!" Catty finished with two thumbs up. She was ready. Not even fussy Opie could bother her today. She knew just what she needed to do.

- 🐾 Apologize to Bebe.
- 🐾 Have a good catitude if Milo decided to be rude again.
- 🐾 Be on her very best behavior for Mr. Grole.

"Catty! Guess what!" Jo said.

Catty jumped and then kneaded her hands together to help her stay chiller than a kitty playing with catnip. "What's up, Jo?"

"I found a rock shaped like my dad's *head!*" She held up an egg-shaped rock. Catty had never seen Jo's dad's head, so she'd have to take her word for it. "Can you believe it? Hey, by the way, is your tail okay after it got stepped on yesterday?"

"My tail is just fine," Catty told her. "Sometimes I even step on it and scare myself."

Jo chuckled. "I guess that would make you a scaredy-cat!"

Catty froze. She didn't know whether to laugh or not. Was Jo making fun of her?

But then Jo broke into a smile. "I'm just playing. I trip over my own feet all the time. I don't know how you do it with two feet *and* a tail. My first day of school was a mess too. Milo gave me a wet willy while the class was watching a movie and I hopped out of my seat, screamed bloody murder, and spilled my whole pencil case!"

"As long as you landed on your feet," Catty said with a smile, thinking about the Scratch Pad and what Granny Tabby's Mama told her when *she* was little.

"Hey, I like that! Did you come up with it on your own? Is it your own personal motto?"

Catty grinned. "Something like that."

"You're so interesting," Jo said. "You should have your own podcast, or a column in the newspaper. My aunt used to work at the newspaper, but she got fired for stealing air fresheners. She didn't need them. She just did it for fun. Now she leaves comments on all the newspaper articles listing out their grammar and spelling mistakes. For fun."

"Your aunt has an interesting idea of fun," Catty told her. If Jo was this offbeat, Catty couldn't even imagine what the rest of her family was like. "Hey, Jo, I'm sorry about what Milo did to you on your first day of school. So gross. And annoying!"

"He's . . . he's a challenge. What can I say? But I feel like growing up with so many little siblings was basically boot camp for dealing with kids like Milo," said Jo.

"Well, I'm an only child," said Catty. "Hey, did Bebe say anything after I left yesterday?"

"About what?"

"About me, well, biting her?" Catty asked, feeling a bit embarrassed. "I just hope she can forgive me. Do you know if she was really hurt?"

"Oh, *that!* About a million things happened yesterday. We went to art class and made wind chimes out of old bottle caps, but before that I broke my pencil in the sharpener and it got jammed so no one else could sharpen—" Jo stopped talking, like she'd suddenly remembered Catty's question, and blushed. "Sorry about that. I get carried away sometimes. Bebe went to see the nurse and came back with a bright pink Band-Aid. No bacon Band-Aid, though. The school just has the basics. I heard she got a Popsicle, too, so you basically did her a favor."

"Well, I wouldn't go *that* far," Catty said. But she was glad to hear that Bebe got a treat out of the ordeal. Hurting anyone, especially when she didn't mean to, ate her up inside.

The bus rolled to a stop and the driver opened the door.

"Day two," Catty said, with her backpack tucked under her arm. "It's meow or never."

She climbed the steps behind Jo and was immediately overwhelmed by all the yelling and laughing again. A balled-up piece of paper flew past her head and Catty pushed away the urge to swat at it.

No hissing, no scratching, no biting.

She really had to do everything right today. No pressure or anything! Ugh.

Except Milo was sitting right in the front row, and gave her a mean stare. Would he lash out at her for hissing at him yesterday? Milo snarled at Catty and buried his face in a comic book.

"We can sit right here," Jo said, pointing to a bench a few rows back.

Catty sat down as the bus lurched forward and began rumbling down the street.

Just like yesterday, Catty felt like the noise and the movement of the bus might be too much for her. The bus driver hummed and whistled as he drove, and the old engine vibrated constantly as the tires hit pothole after pothole.

Catty's tail began to bristle. All the sounds and feelings made her want to scratch something and go cattywampus! She felt like she could sink her nails into the back of the bus driver's seat and shred it to pieces.

But instead she concentrated on the floor beneath her feet, and how solid it felt. How safe she was on the top level of her cat tree back at home.

Then Catty remembered. The Scratch Pad!

She pulled the book out of her backpack, then scraped her nails over the furry cover. It felt good. *Really* good. Oh yeah! Catty was already starting to feel better.

"That's a pretty cool notebook," Jo said. "You know I love a fuzzy notebook! Where'd you get it?"

"My family." Catty smiled. "It's my Scratch Pad."

The rest of the ride to school was still loud and bumpy, but to Catty's surprise, she didn't seem to mind it so much. She made biscuits on the fuzzy cover as Jo chattered on about wind chimes and broken pencils.

Maybe yesterday was just a rehearsal and today could be her real first day of school, because so far things were off to a pawesome start.

CHAPTER TEN

Today, Catty was ready for the buzzing, clanging noise of the morning bell when it rang. It still made her jump a little bit, but in a funny way.

She hurried to class, following Jo, as her tail started bristling. She didn't want to be late, and she knew she was going to see Bebe. This was the moment she'd been waiting for—her big apology! Last night, after bedtime, she stood on her bed like it was a stage and rehearsed exactly what she should say. Waffles was her only audience, but he seemed to be very impressed.

"Good morning, class!" Mr. Grole said when everyone settled down. "Today is a new day! We're starting with math since our map is currently ... unavailable." He gestured helplessly to the ripped-up map, piled in a corner of the room.

Catty sank in her chair. Was he making fun of her in front of the whole class? Rude!

But then he laughed, and Catty could smile at herself with a sigh of relief. So fur, so good. Catty needed to chill out a little. *Think calm kitty thoughts!* One thing was for sure: She would feel much better after apologizing. But Bebe wasn't in class yet.

Was she avoiding Catty? Was she home sick . . . or injured?

Catty tried to focus on math, but was having trouble caring about addition and subtraction, even though at home she loved helping her dad convert and measure ingredients.

"Math is my best subject," Jo whispered to Catty. "I'm so good that my mom lets me count the money in the register at her salon every night."

Catty was impressed. Maybe Jo could help double count her birthday money before the book fair.

Mr. Grole reached into his pocket and Catty flinched. Not the laser pointer again! Her ears shot up on high alert and she almost shut her eyes so she couldn't even be tempted by the sweet, sweet red dot . . .

But instead, he took out a short metal rod and pulled on the end. It expanded into a long pointing stick. "I thought I would give the laser pointer a break," he said with a toothy smile.

Phew!

"Now, who wants to read out our word problem?" Mr. Grole asked, swinging his pointer stick.

Time seemed to slow down. Catty's tail twitched.

As Mr. Grole angled toward the board, the stick made a wide arc, a swooshing sound, then . . .

Thwack!

It hit Douglas Snickerdoodle's fish bowl.

The poor fishy saw it coming and blew a bubble, his mouth puckering into a horrified O.

"Not my darling fish, Douglas Snickerdoodle!" Mr. Grole cried, lunging forward.

He was far too slow to come to the rescue. But lucky for Douglas Snickerdoodle, someone in this third-grade classroom was *extra* fast. And that someone was Catty Corner.

Faster than you could snap your fingers, Catty leapt out of her seat. The class watched in horror as Douglas Snickerdoodle's bowl tipped over, spilling water and Douglas Snickerdoodle over the edge of Mr. Grole's desk.

Jo gasped.

Milo shielded his eyes with his hands. "I can't look!"

Bebe chose that exact moment to walk into the room. "Sorry I'm late—"

Douglas Snickerdoodle's fins flapped helplessly through the air.

"She's going to eat our class pet!" one girl screamed.

Catty ignored her and slid across the floor with her palms open. Just in time to safely catch Douglas Snickerdoodle. The goldfish landed softly in her hands, and Catty jumped to her feet. "You're safe with me, little guy," she told him.

"Nice catch," Bebe said coolly.

"Thanks," Catty said, her breath a little short after all the action.

Mr. Grole set the fish bowl right-side up and Jo fetched some water from the drinking fountain. Working together, they quickly restored Douglas Snickerdoodle's habitat. Catty gently put him back in and he immediately did a celebratory lap around his bowl as if to say, *Thanks for the fin-tastic save, Catty!*

"That was a close call," Mr. Grole said. "But you really saved the day, Catty! You're a real angelfish."

"How did you even *do* that?" To Catty's surprise, it was Milo asking. He still looked like he'd eaten something sour, but at least his question wasn't rude.

Catty shrugged. She hadn't thought about it. That was the not-so-great thing about Tail Intuition, but sometimes it was the pawesome thing instead. "I guess it was my cat-like reflexes."

Milo stared at her for a moment, and then he snickered. Soon the whole class was laughing, even Mr. Grole. Catty herself couldn't help but giggle too.

It took pretty much all morning for everyone to settle down after the drama of Douglas Snickerdoodle's near-death. Finally, Mr. Grole told them it was time for independent study and the students were allowed to read, draw, or write.

Catty pulled out her trusty Scratch Pad and started recounting her day. This was a memory she *never* wanted to forget.

Dear Diary,

Today I felt like a superhero, and I sort of was if you think about it. I saved the class pet fish from certain death, and the only reason I was fast enough to rescue him was because I'm half-cat. Imagine if I hadn't been there! Poor Douglas Snickerdoodle would have gone SPLAT! But I was there. I took a leap, and landed on my feet.

I'm glad I came back to school after my disastrous first day. Maybe a half-cat, half-girl is just what this place needs.

Peace, Love, Paws
(and, sometimes, Claws),
Catty

CHAPTER ELEVEN

It was *finally* lunchtime, and Catty was ready to chow down. But first she had something very important to do. (Yes, there were actually things more important than lunch.)

Jo followed as Catty led the way straight to Bebe's table. Day two of school was already so much better than day one, and Bebe had complimented her quick thinking, but what if she was still upset with Catty? There was only one way to find out.

"Hi, Bebe," Catty said softly as she sat down next to her.

Bebe wore a stylish jumpsuit and sunglasses so big they took up her whole face. Without a doubt, she was the hippest person Catty had ever met. (Not that she'd met many people at all.) Sure enough, there was a pink Band-Aid on Bebe's hand right where Catty had bitten her. Looking at it, Catty almost lost her nerve. She had to make it right, though, even if they didn't end up being friends after all.

"I know I'm probably not your favorite half-cat, half-girl right now," Catty said. "But I just wanted to tell you that I am so sorry for biting you."

"It did hurt pretty bad..." Bebe said as she looked down at her bandage.

Catty felt awful. She really hadn't meant to hurt Bebe. "I really am sorry. Sometimes when things startle me, like when my tail gets stepped on, I just react. Sometimes I howl and sometimes I hiss. And sometimes I scratch and bite, but I'm really trying to get used to school and all of the new things here. I never want to bite or hurt anyone again."

"Thank you for your apology." Bebe smiled a little. "And I get it. Sometimes when I get mad, I say mean things. Which is sort of like biting but with words. I probably wouldn't have been very nice about someone stepping on my tail if I had one, which, by the way is *très chic*."

Catty beamed and then whispered, "I don't actually know what that means."

Bebe leaned toward her. "It's French for 'very stylish.'"

No one had ever called Catty stylish. She tried hard to play it cool. Wait till Waffles heard this!

"I *did* get this awesome fuchsia Band-Aid though," Bebe said. "And fuchsia is *the* color right now according to my older cousin."

"Remind me to visit the nurse's office," Catty said with a grin. "I hear she has Popsicles."

"But not sushi flavor," Bebe said. "That would be magical."

"Or anchovy!"

Jo made a face. "Yuck, you guys."

Bebe held out her hand for Catty to shake. "Friends?"

"Friends!" Catty said, taking Bebe's hand as gently as she could.

"Friends! *PURRR*-EVER!" said Jo in a loud, goofy voice, and she wrapped them both in a big, messy hug. "I mean, if that's okay with you guys..."

Bebe and Catty laughed themselves silly. Catty didn't even mind being swept up into the out-of-nowhere hug. Sometimes surprises felt nice.

"Well, I could really use a friend or two," Catty said.

"The number three is very in right now," Bebe explained. "I like the sound of a trio."

"Hey, why did the cats ask for a drum set?" asked Jo.

Catty and Bebe both shrugged.

Jo played the air drums and said, "So they can make *meow*sic!"

Bebe laughed so hard that her grapefruit-flavored sparkling water shot out her nose. Jo was bowled over, giggling at her own joke, and Catty used her tail to wipe the tears from her eyes.

Catty had to admit: Waffles never had jokes this good.

CHAPTER TWELVE

The book fair was even better than Catty had dreamed. There were tables and tables of books stacked on top of each other in impossibly tall towers.

The whole class lined up in the hallway. Everyone was antsy, not just Catty. Finally, Mr. Grole waved them in.

Catty scampered inside to behold all the books. Her eyes almost popped out of her skull. SO. MANY. BOOKS. SO. LITTLE. TIME.

Catty's tail quivered with excitement. There were books about world record holders, and princesses who slayed dragons, and even galaxies light-years away.

"Best day *ever!*" Jo cried, like she'd just landed on the moon.

"Shhh!" the librarian said with a smile.

The library was bright and quiet except for whispering students and the sound of turning pages. There were even beanbags! Catty could imagine herself curling up with a book in a patch of sunlight. This place was definitely Catty's new home away from home.

"Where do we even begin?" Jo asked.

"At the beginning, I guess," Bebe said. "They have even more stickers this year. Is there any such thing as too many stickers?"

Catty browsed each table. She picked up and touched every book. She would take them all if she could, but these paws could only carry so much.

Mr. Grole walked up beside her and read the back of a book titled *One Hundred Funny Bear Jokes.*

Catty raised an eyebrow. The bear on the cover definitely looked like he could be Mr. Grole's long-lost cousin. Catty wondered if there were any furry friends in his family tree . . .

"Catty, I want to thank you again for saving Douglas Snickerdoodle today," he said. "You know, sometimes students take him home on the weekends to watch him. Maybe you'd like to do that one day."

"Really?" Catty asked. "I eat a lot of fish, though. Do you think he'd be offended?"

Mr. Grole laughed, his voice deep and rumbly. "I think as long as you didn't eat *him,* it would be okay. I'm a big fan of salmon myself."

Catty brought her fingers to her lips and gave a chef's kiss. "You have very good taste."

"Enjoy the book fair." Mr. Grole held up the joke book. "I'm so excited about this one, I can hardly . . . bear it."

Catty continued to roam and her stack of books grew so high that she would've had a hard time balancing everything if it weren't for her excellent feline instincts. She carefully put one foot in front of the other like she was at home balancing on the banister.

Catty roamed into the fantasy section for the latest How to Train Your Troll book. A boy stood by the rack reading a copy of book three, *Trolls in Space*.

"I love that series!" Catty said. "I can't wait for the movie!"

The boy lowered his book. Ugh. Milo. She should have known that red hair anywhere.

Catty's tail puffed out, waiting for him to say something hiss-worthy.

"Yeah," said Milo, looking a bit uncertain. "It's basically the most life-changing series ever." He shrugged. "Did you read the first two?"

Milo was not on her list of favorite people, but she could at least try to be polite to him. "Yes—I love them. I haven't read that one yet, though," Catty said, nodding at the book in his hands.

"I have *The Troll Trainers' Companion*, if you ever want to borrow it. It gives you all the character backstories and even has some bonus artwork. You could come across the street to my house and get it. Just try not to scratch up the pages," he said with a snort.

He was teasing, but it didn't feel mean this time.

"I guess that will depend on how good the book is," Catty told him with a smirk and a fake hiss.

Milo laughed and Catty got back to shopping. *Well, that wasn't awful,* she thought to herself.

Catty finished buying her books. They all fit in her backpack, even if the zipper was basically screaming "HELP ME!"

Jo came up to her in the hallway, clutching five fuzzy journals. "Look! They're just like yours! You inspired me!"

At the end of the day, Catty practically floated down to the bus area. Jo was busy scribbling in a journal. She held a guide to beekeeping under her arm. Bebe had a raft of cookbooks from cultures across the world and even a book about the history of fashion.

The three of them boarded the bus. Catty was eager to get home and write in her diary about the rest of her second day of school. She was grateful she'd taken the leap and given school a second chance. This was only the beginning! From where Catty was sitting—in the rumbly bus—the paw-sibilities seemed endless.

Dear Diary,

Sometimes just when you think everything's gone wrong, you meet a friend or two who show you that it's never too late for a second chance. I can't wait for Waffles to meet Jo and Bebe. I hope he makes a better impression on them than I did on my first day.

I just found out I get to start volunteering in the pre-K classroom every afternoon! Also, Mr. Grole opened his lunch box today and his pudding was missing! No one confessed to eating it, but if you ask me, Milo looked suspicious.

On the way home from school today, Opie the neighbor cat was sitting on the sidewalk and he let me PET him. He even purred! Can you believe that? I guess even old cats really can learn new tricks! Who would've thought?

Until later...

Peace, Love, and Paws,
Catty

union
square
kids

NEW YORK

ISBN 978-1-4549-5647-1 (hardcover)
ISBN 978-1-4549-5648-8 (paperback)
ISBN 978-1-4549-5877-2 (ebook)

Library of Congress Cataloging-in-Publication Data

Names: Murphy, Julie, 1985- author. | Farb, Eve, illustrator.
Title: Catty Corner lands on her feet / by Julie Murphy ; illustrated by Eve Farb.
Description: New York : Union Square Kids, 2025. | Series: Catty corner
Audience: Ages 6-8. | Summary: "Half-cat, half-human Catty Corner navigates the
challenges of beginning third grade—Provided by publisher.
Identifiers: LCCN 2024006019 (print) | LCCN 2024006020 (ebook)
ISBN 9781454956471 (hardcover) | ISBN 9781454956488 (trade paperback)
ISBN 9781454958772 (epub)
Subjects: CYAC: Cats—Fiction. | Schools—Fiction. | Friendship—Fiction. | Family life—Fiction.
Classification: LCC PZ7.M95352 Cat 2025 (print) | LCC PZ7.M95352 (ebook) | DDC [Fic]—dc23
LC record available at https://lccn.loc.gov/2024006019
LC ebook record available at https://lccn.loc.gov/2024006020

For information about custom editions, special sales, and premium purchases,
please contact specialsales@unionsquareandco.com.

Printed in China
Lot #:
2 4 6 8 10 9 7 5 3 1
11/24

unionsquareandco.com

Cover and interior design by Amelia Mack
Cover and interior art by Eve Farb